Contents

Some words are shown in bold, **like this**. You can find out what they mean by looking in the Glossary.

Dogs

I like dogs.

C4 523699 00 E7

NEWCASTLE LIBRARIES

I Like Dogs

NEWCASTLE LIBRARIES	
C452369900	
Bertrams	11/02/2009
J636.7	£5.25

Angela Aylmore

www.heinemann.co.uk/library
Visit our website to find out more information about Heinemann Library books.

To order:
☎ Phone 44 (0) 1865 888066
📄 Send a fax to 44 (0) 1865 314091
💻 Visit the Heinemann Bookshop at www.heinemann.co.uk/library to browse our catalogue and order online.

First published in Great Britain by Heinemann Library, Halley Court, Jordan Hill, Oxford OX2 8EJ, part of Harcourt Education. Heinemann is a registered trademark of Harcourt Education Ltd.

© Harcourt Education Ltd 2007
First published in paperback 2008
The moral right of the proprietor has been asserted.

All rights reserved. No part of this publication may be reproduced, stored in a retrieval system, or transmitted in any form or by any means, electronic, mechanical, photocopying, recording, or otherwise, without either the prior written permission of the publishers or a licence permitting restricted copying in the United Kingdom issued by the Copyright Licensing Agency Ltd, 90 Tottenham Court Road, London W1T 4LP (www.cla.co.uk).

Editorial: Dan Nunn and Sarah Chappelow
Design: Joanna Hinton-Malivoire
Picture research: Erica Newbery
Production: Duncan Gilbert

Origination: Chroma Graphics (Overseas) Pte. Ltd
Printed and bound in China, China by South China Printing Co. Ltd.

ISBN 978 0 431 10958 9 (hardback)
11 10 09 08 07
10 9 8 7 6 5 4 3 2 1

ISBN 978 0 431 10967 1 (paperback)
12 11 10 09 08
10 9 8 7 6 5 4 3 2 1

British Library Cataloguing in Publication Data
Aylmore, Angela
 I like dogs. - (Things I like)
 1. Dogs - Juvenile literature
 I. Title
 636.7
A full catalogue record for this book is available from the British Library.

Acknowledgements
The publishers would like to thank the following for permission to reproduce photographs: Alamy pp. **10** (Dynamic Graphics Group/Creatas), **11** (Colin Hawkins), **18** (Andrew Holt), **22** (dog in bath, Colin Hawkins); Animal Photography p. **7** (Sally Anne Thompson); Corbis pp. **12–13** (Larry Williams), **14–15** (Roy Morsch/zefa), **19** (Jim Craigmyle); Getty Images pp. **4–5** (all, Photodisc); Nature Picture Library pp. **6** (Ulrike Schanz), **8** (Wegner/ARCO), **9** (Wegner, P./ArcoImages), **20** (Ulrike Schanz), **21** (Eric Baccega), **22** (huskies, Eric Baccega; St Bernard, Ulrike Schanz). Cover photograph of a dog reproduced with permission of Corbis (Aaron Horowitz).

Every effort has been made to contact copyright holders of any material reproduced in this book. Any omissions will be rectified in subsequent printings if notice is given to the publishers.

Disclaimer: All the internet addresses (URLs) given in this book were valid at the time of going to press. However, due to the dynamic nature of the internet, some addresses may have changed, or sites ceased to exist since publication. While the author and publishers regret any inconvenience this may cause readers, no responsibility for any such changes can be accepted by either the author or the publishers.

I will tell you my favourite things about dogs.

Different dogs

I like the way dogs are so different. This dog is a St Bernard. It is big and hairy.

This dog is a Peruvian Inca Orchid. It has no hair!

This dog is a dachshund. It is long and short. Some people call it a sausage dog!

I like this dog the best.
It is a Dalmatian. It has
spots all over it.

Taking care of my dog

I really like taking care of my dog. My dog likes to play.

My dog gets very muddy.
I give her a bath to keep
her clean.

I feed my dog every day. I make sure my dog has water to drink.

My dog needs lots of **exercise**. I like to take her for a walk.

Jobs for dogs

I like the way that dogs help people. This dog helps a farmer to look after his sheep.

This is a **guide dog**.

Guide dogs help people
who cannot see.

This dog is a husky.

Huskies work together to pull a sleigh.

Do you like dogs?

Now you know why I like dogs! Do you like dogs too?

Glossary

exercise activity that helps to keep an animal or a human healthy and fit, such as going for a walk

guide dog a dog that helps blind people

Find out more

From Puppy to Dog, Anita Ganeri
(Heinemann Library, 2006)

Looking After Your Pet Dog, Clare Hibbert
(Hodder Wayland, 2005)

Find out everything you need to know about
dogs at: www.loveyourdog.com

Index